For Justin, Jack,
and Harvey

Food Allergies and Me

By Juniper Skinner

This book is intended for initiating allergy awareness conversations with children,
and is not medical advice. **Always consult a doctor with questions and concerns regarding allergies.**

Hi! I'm Jack! I have a little brother, a dragon collection, and I'm pretty good at soccer.

Oh yeah, and I have food allergies.

After breakfast, I'm going to school. Do you want to come too? I can tell you all about having food allergies!

Having allergies means I have to be *super duper* careful, like a mystery detective! If I eat something that I'm allergic to, then I'll get really sick. That's why I investigate food!

I can't eat peanuts.
I can't eat eggs.
And I can't drink milk.

I can't have them because
I'm allergic to them.

Eating food that I'm allergic to can give me spots called hives and make my stomach hurt. Sometimes, they make my throat itchy and I have trouble breathing.

If I feel those things it means I'm having an allergic reaction. And I need to tell a grown up right away! I might have to go to the hospital for medicine.

At school, I'm learning to write my name and sing silly songs. We have rules to follow! Like taking turns and sharing!

We share games and we share toys. But, we never *ever* share food!

Before lunch, we wash all the dirt and germs off our hands! We always wash hands *after* we eat too! That way, nobody touches me with food that I'm allergic to.

Some kids at school have food allergies, just like me! My friend Gabby is allergic to strawberries and Sam can't eat wheat. Sam has an awesome robot lunchbox!

Today is Gabby's birthday! We get to play games and sing to her. My mom even packed a special cupcake for me! Thanks Mom!

Having allergies makes me different from my friends, but we are *all* different in some way.

None of us look alike, we have different kinds of families, and we always have new things to learn from each other!

To stay safe, I have to do lots of things!
I always wear my seat belt, I have a bike
helmet, and I don't eat food that I'm allergic to!

What things do you do to stay safe?

C'mon! We're going to an allergist appointment. My allergy doctor does a test on my back or my arm to see if my allergies are getting better.

I used to get nervous, but now I know it doesn't hurt. It tickles! And it's a little itchy. I always get a sticker or a toy when I'm all done. It's actually pretty cool!

It's time to go to the park! There's a swirly slide and lots of sand. I build magical castles for my dragons! My little brother would swing all day if Mom let him.

Sometimes people try to share snacks with me but I just say, "No thank you"! They're trying to be nice, but having allergies means it's not safe to share food. We always bring our own anyway!

At dinner, I try to eat all my vegetables.
And I take a vitamin every day.
I feel bigger already!

Well, thanks for playing with me today.
Did you have fun?
I sure am sleepy!

Just remember, if you have food allergies or if you have a friend who does, it's okay!

Learning about allergies keeps us all safe and healthy. That makes me feel really happy!

The End

Made in the USA
San Bernardino, CA
25 March 2013